George-isms

The 110 Rules

George Washington Wrote When He Was 14

—and Lived by All His Life

George-
isms

by George Washington

Atheneum Books for Young Readers

New York   London   Toronto   Sydney   Singapore

Atheneum Books for Young Readers
An imprint of Simon & Schuster Children's Publishing Division
1230 Avenue of the Americas
New York, New York 10020

The text of this book is set in Palatino.

Printed in Mexico

2   4   6   8   10   9   7   5   3   1

Library of Congress Cataloging-in-Publication Data
Washington, George, 1732-1799.

[Rules of civility]

George-isms: the 110 rules George Washington wrote when he was 14—
and lived by all his life / by George Washington.—1st ed.

p. cm.

Summary: Presents 110 quotations about civility and behavior
that George Washington copied when he was fourteen years old
and attempted to live by.
ISBN 0-689-84082-9

1. Washington, George, 1732-1799—Quotations—Juvenile literature.
2. Conduct of life—quotations, maxims, etc.—Juvenile literature.
[1. Washington, George, 1732-1799—Quotations. 2. Conduct of life.]
I. Title.

E312.79.R85 2000

973.4'1'092—dc21   00-026763

For his help preparing this volume, the publisher wishes to thank
John Rhodehamel, Norris Foundation Curator of American Historical
Manuscripts, Huntington Library, San Marino, California.

Washington's *110 Rules of Civility and Decent Behaviour* were collected
and promulgated in France by Jesuit teachers, their first appearance being in
1595; in 1640 they were translated into English by Francis Hawkins. Scholars
disagree on how they reached Virginia in the 1700s, but their importance in
Washington's life is undisputed.

For more about the Rules, see *Rules of Civility; the 110 Precepts That
Guided our First President in War and Peace*, edited by Richard Brookhiser (New
York: Free Press, 1997) and *George Washington's Rules of Civility and Decent
Behaviour*, edited by Charles Moore (Boston: 1926).

Introduction

NOT SO VERY LONG AGO, a teenaged boy in Virginia dreamed of great things. He was smart, good with numbers, tall for his age. He studied hard at school. He could not have known where his life would lead him, but he did know one thing: he would have a bright future.

One of his teachers—or perhaps his father—presented him with a list of one-hundred-ten rules for living. Some of the rules were less useful than others, but they meant a lot to this ambitious boy. He wrote out the rules in his own handwriting and kept them with him—and tried his best to follow them—all his life.

The boy was George Washington, and his intelligence, leadership, and vision took him from the farmlands of Virginia to the battle-fields of the Revolution and eventually, to the first presidency of the United States. But Washington's gentility and courtesy were also part of his success. He knew how to talk to heads of state and common soldiers; he knew how to behave in royal courts and local taverns. The rules of civility and decent behavior that he had copied down at age fourteen were a standard he tried to live up to all his life.

George-isms provides young readers the full text of Washington's original one-hundred-ten rules, as well as a "translation" into modern vernacular English. Some of the rules will sound funny and out-of-date. But many of them—the best of them—still provide for modern Americans the kind of moral and ethical guidance that steered the character of our Founding Father.

And who knows? Maybe some girls or boys reading this today will find in *George-isms* some words to live by—words that might take them all the way to the White House.

✪ ✪ ✪

George-isms

1st

✪ ✪ ✪

EVERY action done in company ought to be with some sign of respect to those that are present.

RESPECT others.

2nd

✪ ✪ ✪

WHEN in company, put not your hands to any part of the body, not usually discovered.

DON'T fidget or scratch your private parts in public.

3rd

✪ ✪ ✪

SHOW nothing to your friend that may affright him.

DON'T scare or worry your friends.

4th

✪ ✪ ✪

IN the presence of others sing not to yourself with a humming noise, nor drum with your fingers or feet.

DON'T hum when people are around, or bang your fingers on the table.

5th

✪ ✪ ✪

IF you cough, sneeze, sigh, or yawn, do it not loud but privately; and speak not in your yawning, but put your handkerchief or hand before your face and turn aside.

DON'T make a lot of noise when you cough, sneeze, sigh, or yawn; don't talk through your yawn, and cover your mouth with a tissue.

6th

✪ ✪ ✪

SLEEP not when others speak, sit not when others stand, speak not when you should hold your peace, walk not on when others stop.

KEEP pace with your friends.

7th

✪ ✪ ✪

PUT not off your clothes in the presence of others, nor go out your chamber half dressed.

DON'T go around half dressed.

8th

✪ ✪ ✪

AT play and at fire it is good manners to give place to the last comer, and affect not to speak louder than ordinary.

IF someone wants to join your game or needs a warm place to sit, give her a chance; also, don't talk too loud.

9th

✪ ✪ ✪

SPIT not in the fire, nor stoop low before it. Neither put your hands into the flames to warm them, nor set your feet upon the fire, especially if there be meat before it.

DON'T spit in the kitchen, and don't put your hands too close to a flame.

10th

☻ ☻ ☻

WHEN you sit down, keep your feet firm and even, without putting one on the other or crossing them.

KEEP your feet on the floor when you're sitting down.

11th

☻ ☻ ☻

SHIFT not yourself in the sight of others nor gnaw your nails.

DON'T wiggle around when people are talking to you, and don't bite your nails.

12th

✪ ✪ ✪

SHAKE not the head, feet, or legs; roll not the eyes; lift not one eyebrow higher than the other; wry not the mouth; and bedew no man's face with your spittle by approaching too near him when you speak.

DON'T make weird faces at people, and when you get excited, make sure you're not spitting on anyone.

13th

✪ ✪ ✪

KILL no vermin as fleas, lice, ticks &c in the sight of others; if you see any filth or thick spittle, put your foot dexteriously upon it; if it be upon the clothes of your companions, put it off privately; and if it be upon your own clothes, return thanks to him who puts it off.

DON'T squish bugs around other people; and if there's gunk on your friend's clothes, take it

off when people aren't looking; also, if someone
takes gunk off your clothes, thank him for doing it.

14th

✪ ✪ ✪

TURN not your back to others especially in speaking; jog not the table or desk on which another reads or writes; lean not upon any one.

DON'T turn your back when someone's talking to you; don't jiggle a table if someone's reading or writing on it; and don't lean on other people.

15th

✪ ✪ ✪

KEEP your nails clean and short, also your hands and teeth clean, yet without showing any great concern for them.

KEEP your nails short and clean, and your hands clean; but don't be vain about it.

16th

✪ ✪ ✪

DO not puff up the cheeks; loll not out the tongue, rub the hands, or beard, thrust out the lips, or bite them, or keep the lips too open or close.

DON'T do weird stuff with your mouth.

17th

✪ ✪ ✪

BE no flatterer; neither play with any that delights not to be played with.

DON'T flatter people, and don't tease people who don't like to be teased.

18th

✪   ✪   ✪

READ no letters, books, or papers in company; but when there is a necessity for the doing of it, you must ask leave. Come not near the books or writings of another so as to read them or give your opinion of them unasked; also look not nigh when another is writing a letter.

DON'T read when other people are talking to you; if you have to read in the presence of others, ask them if they'll excuse you for a minute. And don't look over people's shoulders when they're reading or writing or give them your opinion of what you've read.

19th

✪   ✪   ✪

LET your countenance be pleasant, but in serious matters somewhat grave.

SMILE when things are good; keep a straight face when people are talking about serious matters.

20th

✪ ✪ ✪

THE gestures of the body must be suited to the discourse you are upon.

THE way you gesture with your hands should match what you're talking about.

21st

✪ ✪ ✪

REPROACH none for the infirmities of nature, nor delight to put them that have in mind thereof.

DON'T be mean to people about how they look, don't call attention to other people's problems, and if someone's not as lucky as you are, don't rub it in.

22nd

✪ ✪ ✪

SHOW not yourself glad at the misfortune of another, though he were your enemy.

BE a good sport, even with people you don't like.

23rd

✪ ✪ ✪

WHEN you see a crime punished, you may be inwardly pleased, but always show pity to the suffering offender.

WHEN someone gets in trouble for doing something wrong, it's okay to feel that justice has been done; but always be sensitive to the one who's being punished.

24th

✪ ✪ ✪

DO not laugh too much or too loud in public.

DO not laugh too much or too loud in public.

25th

✪ ✪ ✪

SUPERFLUOUS compliments and all affectation of ceremony are to be avoided, yet where due, they are not to be neglected.

DON'T kiss up to people, but when a friend deserves a compliment, give it to him.

26th

✪　✪　✪

IN pulling off your hat to persons of distinction, as noblemen, justices, churchmen, &c, make a reverence, bowing more or less according to the custom of the better bred and quality of the person. Among your equals, expect not always that they should begin with you first, but to pull off your hat when there is no need is affectation; in the matter of saluting and resaluting in words, keep to the most usual custom.

SHOW special respect to people such as teachers and clergy, and remember that people might have different kinds of manners when you're in a new place.

27th

❁ ❁ ❁

'TIS ill manners to bid one more eminent than yourself be covered as well as not to do it to whom it's due; likewise, he that makes too much haste to put on his hat does not well, yet he ought to put it on at the first, or at most the second time of being asked. Now what is herein spoken, of qualification in behavior in saluting, ought to be observed in taking of place, and sitting down for ceremonies without bounds is troublesome.

DON'T ask for signs of respect that you are not willing to give yourself.

28th

✪ ✪ ✪

IF anyone come to speak to you while you are sitting, stand up, though he be your inferior; and when you present seats, let it be to everyone according to his degree.

STAND up when people are talking to you, and make sure that people who need a seat more than you do get one.

29th

✪ ✪ ✪

WHEN you meet with one of greater quality than yourself, stop, and retire, especially if it be a door or any straight place to give way for him to pass.

IT'S polite to let others go ahead of you.

30th

✪ ✪ ✪

IN walking, the highest place in most countries seems to be on the right hand, therefore, place yourself on the left of him whom you desire to honor, but if three walk together, the mid place is the most honorable; the wall is usually given to the most worthy if two walk together.

WHEN you're walking with someone, walk to the left of him, if you want to show him respect; if there are three of you, the one you most respect goes in the middle; and next to the wall is the place of honor when you walk along a wall.

31st

✪ ✪ ✪

IF any one far surpasses others, either in age, estate, or merit, yet would give place to one meaner than himself in his own lodging, the one ought not to accept it; so he, on the other hand, should not use much earnestness nor offer it above once or twice.

IF someone who doesn't have the means offers to let you stay in his house, you should refuse; and if you're the one doing the offering, just do it once or twice and bow out gracefully if the person turns down your offer.

32nd

✪ ✪ ✪

TO one that is your equal, or not much inferior, you are to give the chief place in your lodging; and he to who it is offered ought at first to refuse it, but at the second accept, though not without acknowledging his own unworthiness.

IF someone is staying at your house, you should offer her the best place; she should first say no, then yes, and be grateful about it.

33rd

✪ ✪ ✪

THEY that are in dignity or in office have in all places precedency; but whilst they are young, they ought to respect those that are their equals in birth or other qualities, though they have no public charge.

PEOPLE in government deserve the highest respect; but they in turn should respect those who are older and wiser than they.

34th

✪ ✪ ✪

IT is good manners to prefer them to whom we speak before ourselves, especially if they be above us with whom in no sort we ought to begin.

LET others go ahead of you in conversation, especially if they particularly deserve respect.

35th

✪ ✪ ✪

LET your discourse with men of business be short and comprehensive.

WHEN you're talking about business, be short and to the point.

36th

✪ ✪ ✪

ARTIFICERS & persons of low degree ought not to use many ceremonies to Lords or others of high degree, but respect and highly honor them; and those of high degree ought to treat them with affability & courtesy, without arrogance.

WHEN you're talking to people older or wiser than you, don't make a big deal out of their superiority; conversely, people who are superior to you should treat you with respect.

37th

✪ ✪ ✪

IN speaking to men of quality, do not lean nor look them full in the face, nor approach too near them, at least keep full place from them.

WHEN you talk to people you admire, don't talk right in their faces or stand too close to them.

38th

✪ ✪ ✪

IN visiting the sick, do not presently play the physician if you be not knowing therein.

WHEN you're with a sick person, don't act like his doctor if you don't know what you're talking about.

39th

✪ ✪ ✪

IN writing or speaking, give every person his due title according to his degree & the custom of the place.

WHEN you're writing or talking to people, make sure you call them "Mr." or "Ms." or whatever they ask that you call them.

40th

✪ ✪ ✪

STRIVE not with your superiors in argument, but always submit your judgement to others with modesty.

IF people know more than you do, you shouldn't argue with them, and if you know more than other people, you don't need to be conceited about it.

41st

✪ ✪ ✪

UNDERTAKE not to teach your equal in the art himself professes, it savours of arrogance.

IT'S pretty arrogant to assume you can teach a friend something he already knows.

42nd

✪ ✪ ✪

LET thy ceremonies in courtesy be proper to the dignity of his place with who thou converses, for it is absurd to act the same with a clown and a prince.

THE way you act with your friends should be different than the way you act with people in authority.

43rd

✪ ✪ ✪

DO not express joy before one sick or in pain, for that contrary passion will aggravate his misery.

BE sensitive to the feelings of those who are sick or in pain; your happy mood might make them feel worse.

44th

✪ ✪ ✪

WHEN a man does all he can though it succeeds not well blame not him that did it.

WHEN someone tries his best and doesn't succeed, don't blame him for trying.

45th

✪ ✪ ✪

BEING to advise or reprehend any one, consider whether it ought to be in public or private, presently or at some other time, in what terms to do it; and in reproving show no sign of cholar, but do it with all sweetness and mildness.

IF you're going to criticize someone, think about where and when you're going to do it—in a group or in private—and do it mildly, without getting angry.

46th

✪ ✪ ✪

TAKE all admonitions thankfully in what time or place soever given, but afterwards, not being culpable, take a time & place convenient to let him know it that gave them.

IF you get blamed for something you didn't do, first make sure your conscience is clear; then tell the person who blamed you that you did nothing wrong.

47th

✪ ✪ ✪

MOCK not nor jest at any thing of importance; break no jests that are sharp biting; and if you deliver any thing witty and pleasant, abstain from laughing thereat yourself.

DON'T make fun of things that are important; don't make mean or ugly jokes; don't laugh at your own jokes.

48th

✪ ✪ ✪

WHEREIN you reprove another be unblameable yourself, for example is more prevalent than precepts.

PEOPLE in glass houses shouldn't throw stones; let your actions speak louder than your words.

49th

✪ ✪ ✪

USE no reproachful language against anyone; neither curse nor revile.

DON'T reproach people; don't curse at them or insult them.

50th

❂ ❂ ❂

BE not hasty to believe flying reports to the disparagement of any.

DON'T be too quick to believe a rumor.

51st

❂ ❂ ❂

WEAR not your clothes foul, ripped or dusty, but see that they be brushed once every day, at least, and take heed that you are approach not any uncleanness.

KEEP your clothes in good shape, and stay clean.

52nd

❂ ❂ ❂

IN your apparel be modest and endeavour to accommodate nature; rather than to procure admiration, keep to the fashion of your equals, such as are civil and orderly with respect to times and places.

DON'T dress up too flashily, and don't use your clothes to show off and make others feel bad.

53rd

✪ ✪ ✪

RUN not in the streets; neither go too slowly nor with mouth open; go not shaking your arms; kick not the earth with your feet; go not upon the toes nor in the dancing fashion.

DON'T run in the streets; don't walk too slowly with your mouth open; don't shake your arms around; don't kick a rock with your feet; and don't walk on tiptoe.

54th

✪ ✪ ✪

PLAY not the peacock, looking everywhere about you, to see if you be well decked, if your shoes fit well, if your stockings sit neatly, and clothes handsomely.

DON'T act like a peacock and strut around, comparing your clothes to others'.

55th

✪ ✪ ✪

EAT not in the streets nor in the house out of season.

DON'T eat in the street, and at home, just eat at mealtime.

56th

✪ ✪ ✪

ASSOCIATE yourself with men of good quality, if you esteem your own reputation; for it is better to be alone than in bad company.

BE friends with people you admire; it is better to be alone than in bad company.

57th

✪ ✪ ✪

IN walking up and down in a house, only with one in company if he be greater than yourself, at the first give him the right hand and stop not till he does and be not the first that turns; and when you do turn let it be with your face towards him; if he be a man of great quality, walk not with him cheek by joul, but somewhat behind him, but yet in such a manner that he may easily speak to you.

WHEN you're walking with someone you respect, take your lead from him or her; don't crowd your companion as you walk, either.

58th

✪ ✪ ✪

LET your conversation be without malice or envy, for it is a sign of a tractable and commendable nature; and in all cases of passion admit reason to govern.

IF your goal is to be flexible and pleasant, then don't be mean about other people in conversation; and always be rational.

59th

✪ ✪ ✪

NEVER express anything unbecoming nor act against the rules moral before your inferiors.

DON'T act arrogantly if you're in a position of power.

60th

✪ ✪ ✪

BE not immodest in urging your friends
to discover a secret.

DON'T press your friends into telling you
secrets.

61st

✪ ✪ ✪

UTTER not base and frivolous things amongst grave and learned men; nor very difficult questions or subjects among the ignorant; or with things hard to be believed, stuff not your discourse with sentences, amongst your betters nor equals.

DON'T joke around with serious people, especially teachers; don't bring up subjects that other people don't understand; when you're trying to convince someone of something, don't keep talking and talking.

62nd

✪ ✪ ✪

SPEAK not of doleful things in a time of mirth or at the table; speak not of melancholy things as death and wounds, and if others mention them, change if you can the discourse. Tell not your dreams but to your intimate friends.

WHEN people are having a good time, don't bring up depressing subjects, and if someone else does, try to change the subject. Only tell your dreams to your good friends.

63rd

✪ ✪ ✪

A man ought not to value himself of his achievements or rare qualities of wit, much less of his riches, virtue or kindred.

DON'T boast about your achievements or your own intelligence, and especially not about your money, your good deeds, or your family.

64th

✪ ✪ ✪

BREAK not a jest where none take plea-
sure in mirth; laugh not aloud, nor at all
without occasion; deride no man's misfortune, though there seems to be some
cause.

*DON'T clown around when everyone is
being serious. Don't laugh at someone else's
mistakes, even if you think it's deserved.*

65th

SPEAK not injurious words, neither in jest or earnest; scoff at none although they give occasion.

DON'T say hurtful things, either as a tease or in earnest; don't make fun of others, even if you think they deserve it.

66th

BE not forward but friendly and courteous; be the first to salute, hear, and answer; & be not pensive when it's time to converse.

DON'T go overboard, but do be friendly and courteous; be the first to say hello, listen, and answer; and don't brood silently when it's time to talk.

67th

✪ ✪ ✪

DETRACT not from others; neither be
excessive in commanding.

*DON'T cut people down; don't boss people
around.*

68th

✪ ✪ ✪

GO not thither, where you know not, whether you shall be welcoming or not. Give not advice without being asked & when desired do it briefly.

DON'T go places you're not welcome. Don't give advice unless you're asked, and keep it brief.

69th

✪ ✪ ✪

IF two contend together, take not the part of either unconstrained; and be not obstinate in your own opinion; in things indifferent be of the major side.

DON'T take sides; don't stubbornly cling to your opinion just because it's yours; when you don't care either way, go with the majority.

70th

❂ ❂ ❂

REPREHEND not the imperfections of others, for that belongs to parents, masters, and superiors.

DON'T try to fix people's faults—leave that to parents and teachers.

71st

❂ ❂ ❂

GAZE not on the marks or blemishes of others and ask not how they came. What you may speak in secret to your friend, deliver not before others.

DON'T stare at people's scars and blemishes, and don't ask about them. If you're going to talk about a secret, let someone else bring up the topic first.

72nd

✪ ✪ ✪

SPEAK not in an unknown tongue in company, but in your own language and that as those of quality do and not as the vulgar. Sublime matters treat seriously.

DON'T use slang that other people won't understand; don't use gross language. Treat important matters seriously.

73rd

✪ ✪ ✪

THINK before you speak; pronounce not imperfectly nor bring out your words too hastily, but orderly & distinctly.

THINK before you speak; think when you speak, put your thoughts together, and don't talk too fast.

74th

❂ ❂ ❂

WHEN another speaks be attentive yourself and disturb not the audience; if any hesitates in his words, help him not, nor prompt him without desired; interrupt him not, nor answer him till his speech be ended.

LISTEN to people when they're talking to you, and don't distract others; if someone stutters or stumbles in his conversation, don't fill his words in for him; don't interrupt, and let him finish his thought before you make your answer.

75th

❂ ❂ ❂

IN the midst of discourse ask not of what one treateth, but if you perceive any stop because of your coming may well intreat him gently to proceed. If a person of quality comes in while you are conversing, it is handsome to repeat what was said before.

DON'T interrupt a conversation to find out what's being talked about; but if there's a pause, ask then. It's nice to tell a newcomer what your conversation is about when she joins the group.

76th

✪ ✪ ✪

WHILE you are talking, point not with your finger at him of whom you discourse nor approach too near him to whom you talk, especially to his face.

DON'T point, and especially don't point in some-one's face.

77th

✪ ✪ ✪

TREAT with men at fit times about business;
and whisper not in the company of others.

*TALK about business only when it's appropriate;
don't whisper when other people are around.*

78th

✪ ✪ ✪

MAKE no comparisons; and if any of the company be commended for any brave act of
virtue, comment not another for the same.

*DON'T compare one person to another; if someone
is praised for doing a good deed don't use that
moment to praise other people's achievements.*

79th

✪ ✪ ✪

BE not apt to relate news if you know not the truth thereof. In discoursing of things you have heard, name not your author; always a secret discover not.

DON'T spread rumors; don't tell on people; don't tell secrets.

80th

✪ ✪ ✪

BE not tedious in discourse or in reading unless you find the company pleased therewith.

MAKE sure the people you're with don't find you boring when you talk or read aloud.

81st

✪ ✪ ✪

BE not curious to know the affairs of others; neither approach those that speak in private.

DON'T pry into other people's business, and don't eavesdrop on private conversations.

82nd

✪ ✪ ✪

UNDERTAKE not what you cannot perform, but be careful to keep your promise.

DON'T promise more than you can deliver.

83rd

✪ ✪ ✪

WHEN you deliver a matter do it with passion & with discretion, however mean the person be you do it to.

WHEN you take up a task, do it with all your heart, even if there's little reward.

84th

✪   ✪   ✪

WHEN your superiors talk to any body, hearken not neither speak nor laugh.

WHEN your teacher or boss is talking, don't talk or laugh out of turn.

85th

✪   ✪   ✪

IN the company of those of higher quality than yourself, speak not until you are asked a question, then stand upright, put off your hat, & answer in few words.

WHEN you're with someone in authority, speak when you're spoken to, show respect, and be brief.

86th

✪ ✪ ✪

IN disputes, be not so desirous to over-
come as not to give liberty to each one
to deliver his opinion and submit to the
judgement of the major part, especially
if they are judges of the dispute.

WHEN you're having an argument with
someone, don't try to beat him into the
ground; listen to what he has to say and
let the majority rule.

87th

✪　✪　✪

LET thy carriage be such as becomes a man: grave, settled, and attentive to that which is spoken. Contradict not at every turn what others say.

LISTEN closely to what others have to say. Don't tell people they're wrong all the time.

88th

✪ ✪ ✪

BE not tedious in discourse, make not many
disgressions, nor repeat often the same manner
of discourse.

*DON'T be boring when you talk; don't go off on
tangents; and don't tell the same story over and
over again.*

89th

✪ ✪ ✪

SPEAK not evil of the absent, for it is unjust.

DON'T talk behind someone's back. It's not fair.

90th

✪ ✪ ✪

BEING set at meat, scratch not; neither spit, cough, or blow your nose, except if there is a necessity for it.

DON'T scratch, spit, cough, or blow your nose at the table, unless you absolutely have to.

91st

✪ ✪ ✪

MAKE no show of taking great delight in your victuals; feed not with greediness; cut your bread with a knife; lean not on the table; neither find fault with what you eat.

DON'T look too eager to eat; don't stuff your face; cut your bread with a knife; don't lean on the table; don't complain about the food.

92nd

✪ ✪ ✪

TAKE no salt, nor cut your bread with your greasy knife.

DON'T reach into a salt cellar or a serving dish with silverware you've been eating with.

93rd

✪ ✪ ✪

ENTERTAINING anyone at the table it is decent to present him with meat; undertake not to help others undesired by the master.

IF someone is joining you for a meal, it should be a good meal; don't ask guests to a dinner you're not hosting.

94th

✪ ✪ ✪

IF you soak your bread in the sauce, let it be no more than what you put in your mouth at a time; and blow not you mouth at a time; and blow not your broth at table but stay till it cools of itself.

IF you dunk your bread in your gravy, just dunk one mouthful at a time; don't try to cool your food while it's in your mouth; and don't blow on your food—wait till it cools.

95th

✪ ✪ ✪

PUT not your meat to your mouth with your knife in your hand; neither spit forth the stones of any fruit pie upon a dish nor cast anything under the table.

DON'T eat with your knife; and don't spit out stuff onto your plate or onto the floor.

96th

✪ ✪ ✪

IT is unbecoming to stoop too much to one's meat. Keep your fingers clean & when foul, wipe them on a corner of your table napkin.

BRING your food to your mouth, not your mouth to your food. Keep your hands clean by using your napkin.

97th

✪ ✪ ✪

PUT not another bit into you mouth till the former be swallowed. Let not your morsels be too big.

DON'T stuff your mouth; wait till you've finished one bite before you start another.

98th

✪ ✪ ✪

DRINK not, nor talk with your mouth full; neither gaze about you while you are drinking.

DON'T talk when your mouth is full from eating or drinking; and don't stare at people when you're having something to drink.

99th

✪ ✪ ✪

DRINK not too leisurely, nor yet too hastily; before and after drinking, wipe your lips; breath not then or ever with too great a noise, for it is uncivil.

DON'T gulp down your drinks or sip them too long, and always wipe your mouth between sips; don't make lots of noise when you're drinking or other times, it's not polite.

100th

✪ ✪ ✪

CLEANSE not your teeth with the table cloth
napkin, fork, or knife; but if others do it, let it
be done with a pick tooth.

DON'T clean your teeth with your napkin or your
fork or knife; if you have to do it at all, do it with a
toothpick.

101st

✪ ✪ ✪

RINSE not your mouth in the presence of others.

DON'T rinse out your mouth when others are
around.

102nd

✪ ✪ ✪

IT is out of use to call upon the company often to eat; nor need you drink to others every time you drink.

YOU don't always have to toast someone when you sit down to eat or drink.

103rd

✪ ✪ ✪

IN company of your betters, be not longer in eating than they are; lay not your arm but only your hand upon the table.

KEEP pace with everyone as you eat; and keep your elbows off the table.

104th

✪ ✪ ✪

IT belongs to the chiefest in the company to unfold his napkin and fall to meat first, but he ought then to begin in time & to dispatch with dexterity that the slowest may have time allowed him.

THE person in charge of dinner should start eating first and should make sure she gives enough time for everyone to eat, even the slow ones.

105th

✪ ✪ ✪

BE not angry at table whatever happens, and if you have reason to be so, show it not; put on a cheerful countenance especially if there be strangers, for good humor makes one dish of meat a feast.

TRY not to get angry at the dinner table, even if people are arguing; a cheerful group makes a feast out of a snack.

106th

✪ ✪ ✪

SET not yourself at the upper end of the table; but if it be your due or that the master of the house would have it is, contend not, least you should trouble the company.

DON'T sit at the head of the table unless you're asked.

107th

✪ ✪ ✪

IF others talk at the table, be attentive; but talk not with meat in your mouth.

DON'T talk with your mouth full.

108th

✪ ✪ ✪

WHEN you speak of God or his attributes, let it be seriously & with reverence. Honor & obey your natural parents although they be poor.

DON'T take God's name in vain; honor your parents, even if they're not rich.

109th

✪ ✪ ✪

LET your recreations be manful not sinful.

WHEN you're having fun, don't hurt others.

110th

✪　✪　✪

LABOR to keep alive in your breast that little celestial fire called conscience.

WORK on listening to your conscience. It's the spark of your soul.